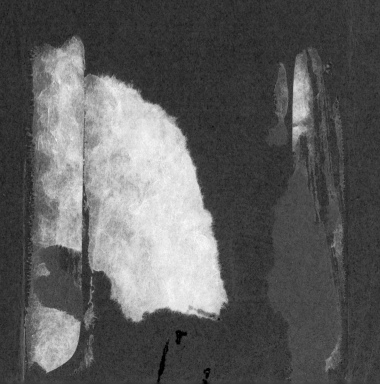

Little Two and the Peach Tree

LITTLE
TWO
and the
PEACH
TREE

PATRICIA MILES
MARTIN

drawings by Joan Berg

ATHENEUM

New York   *1963*

For Nelle, Shirley and Jill Ann

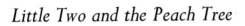

Little Two and the Peach Tree

Peach Blossom,

second child in the House of Ling, sat
in the garden near a sundial, with
paper and sticks of water color. She
was painting a picture of a peach tree.

She moistened the top of the brush
between her lips, laid it upon a stick
of green color, and touched brush to
paper delicately.

As she painted, she looked often at a beautiful peach tree, which grew near the rice fields.

Beyond the peach tree, the narrow fields were plowed and leveled, almost ready for the transplanting of the young rice seedlings.

(4)

This was a wonderful day, for soon the cool water, channeled from river to field, would be released to flood out upon the thirsty earth. And only then would the fields be ready to receive the rice plants.

Father and brother would work ankle deep in mud, directing and helping those who set the seedlings in the soft mud of the fields. And there the rice would grow and thrive until harvest time.

And when harvest came, it would bring all good things to the House of Ling: food—clothing—

And her father would say to Ho, her brother: "We have done well. You will continue to go to your teacher until another harvest. Some day you will be a fine scholar."

(6)

He would say to Peach Blossom, "Little Two, for you there is fine silk for your sewing, a tutor to teach you to play upon the samisen, and sticks of water color."

But he would expect no answer, for Peach Blossom was a child too shy to speak.

For as long as she could remember, she had felt afraid: afraid of new friends, afraid of strange places.

"There is nothing to fear," Ho, her brother, had said. But Peach Blossom had not answered.

Now, her brother came into the garden and stood looking down at her painting.

"Your tree is so true that a kingfisher might well perch upon its painted branch. I have heard that a picture is worth ten thousand words, and I see this is so. I could not describe the beauty you show with your brush."

Peach Blossom felt warm with pleasure. Ho walked on through the garden and ran lightly down the terraced slope of the fields.

Then she saw that her father ran,
too.

He ran heavily along the narrow
footpath that divided the fields, and
he waved his arms and shouted. His
words came on the wind—

"The water from the river does not
flow into the canal."

"No water—"

Her mother came from the house
and looked out toward the fields.
"Why do they shout?" she said.

Again the cry came from the rice
field—

"No water!"—

"This cannot be," her mother said,
"for the river runs high." She hugged
her sleeves. "Without water, the seedlings cannot be transplanted. Without
transplanting, the seedlings will die.
Without rice—"

Without rice.

Peach Blossom shivered, for she remembered a long-ago time when there was no rice. When the river ran low and the rains did not come, then all the people in the valley had gone on the great train which crept toward the city like a black dragon, and they had found new work. When this came to pass, there was no school for Ho, nor watercolors for her, and sometimes but little food and no happiness; for they all waited to return to the land.

(13)

Her father came along the narrow footpath that marked the edge of the fields, and Peach Blossom felt his anger before he spoke.

"That pig of a neighbor on the north has flooded his own fields with river water. His seedlings are planted. But the box which turns the water into our canal has not been opened."

He struck his hands together. "I went on the neighbor's land and saw the box. It is shut securely. I have sent Ho to find out why this is so."

He breathed hard. "For generations the water has flowed freely across that land to ours. And now this man comes to the province, and he acts like a great lord—"

He tramped into the house, and the mother followed. Peach Blossom remained beside the sundial, waiting and watching for Ho's return.

And finally when he did return, she saw that he brought good tidings, for he walked proudly.

He came, a smile wide on his face. "I went to the house of the neighbor," he said. "I pounded on the door, and a fat man answered. I asked for the Master, and he was not there. I asked for paper upon which to write a message to leave for the master."

Peach Blossom saw that Ho was proud to show his learning.

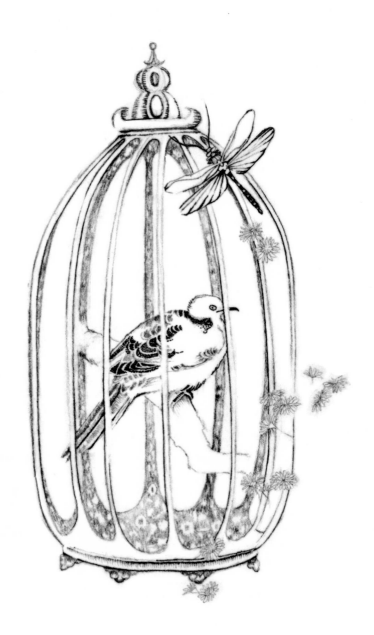

Ho still spoke. "Even before I could give this message to the man, the neighbor returned. He carried a lark in a bamboo cage."

Ho's father came from the house into the garden.

"You gave him the message?" his father asked.

"I gave him the message," Ho answered.

"And then?" his father asked.

"And then we talked of many things; of black dragonflies, of the peach trees that grow in his courtyard, of the lark that sang in its cage."

The father stood with his feet well apart, looking toward the fields.

"Doubtless all will be well. Doubtless he will order the canal to be opened. If this is not done before evening, Ho and I will go together, ourselves, and

(17)

force open the lock which holds back the water. We will go tomorrow before the sun rises.''

That night, Peach Blossom lay down to sleep and watched the pattern which the moonlight painted on the floor beside her. The water had not come. What would happen, she wondered, when morning came.

It seemed she had slept only a short while when she heard her mother preparing the morning rice. It was still dark, and she arose and warmed her hands over the white coals of the brazier.

Soon the rice was prepared, and Ho and his father ate.

When the last grain of rice was eaten, the father set his bowl upon the table.

"The time has come," he said. "We go before the sun rises."

Peach Blossom and her mother watched from the doorway. Ho and his father were two dark figures moving along in the still gray morning.

They walked along the narrow footpath and crossed over upon the neighbor's land while the valley slept.

Then Peach Blossom saw that not all the valley slept, for three dark figures crept through the night; they carried sticks and set upon the two. There was shouting and fighting.

She hid her face in her hands. Dogs barked in the distance, and birds awakened. She felt her mother's gentle hand upon her shoulder.

(21)

"Do not weep, Little Two. No harm is done. Lift your head. Already they return."

Ho and his father came limping into the garden.

"Three men came from the neighbor's house," cried the father. "They would not listen to me. I told them we were there only to turn the river water into our canal, water to which we are entitled."

"They asked why we did not go in the day, like honest men," Ho said.

"Honest men!" the father shouted. "I told them they would find none more honest in the province."

"They did not listen," Ho said, rubbing the top of his head.

"And they had the power of seven men," his father said.

(22)

"No rice—" the mother said softly.

And Peach Blossom touched her mother's hand to comfort her.

They mourned until the sun rose and the valley awakened and all men went to work in the fields, except the men in the House of Ling.

(24)

While they talked together, Peach Blossom slipped away and found the sticks of water color and the painting, where she had left them.

She reached for a stick of brown color and made a few strokes with her brush—harsh strokes this time. There on the lower half of the paper, below the first tree, there came to be a second; it was the same tree, beside a rice field—and the tree was twisted and dead.

(25)

Peach Blossom waited for the color to dry, and then she rolled the paper into a long tube and quietly went from the house.

For a moment, she stood in the garden and she thought of the neighbor's house, knowing she must go there. This she must do for her father and for her mother and for Ho, her brother. Her heart beat as hard and fast as the heart of a captive bird.

Careful not to disturb twig or pebble, she crossed over the flat stones to the road; and then she hurried, afraid that someone would miss her and order her return.

She reached the neighbor's house and opened the moon gate that led into his garden. He was there in the courtyard, a sleeve dog at his feet.

(27)

Peach Blossom was afraid.

She bowed and held the paper toward him.

"What is this?" he said. "What is this?" He unrolled the scroll; and when Peach Blossom did not answer, he looked at her curiously. "I like this," he said. "It is a painting of merit. I observe this has meaning." He waited.

Peach Blossom crossed her hands at her throat and looked down at the earth.

The neighbor spoke again. "You do not answer, child," he said. "Is it that you cannot speak?"

She shook her head, and her face felt hot.

(28)

He looked at the picture again. "The peach tree is beautiful. Far more beautiful than those that grow here in my courtyard. It stands beside a rice field. Perhaps this tree is on your own land."

Peach Blossom bowed.

The neighbor raised an eyebrow. "And below, I see the same tree. It stands beside a field which is prepared for the rice planting, and the tree is twisted and dead, a mere skeleton of the first. Why should this be so?" He stroked the few hairs of his beard.

Peach Blossom opened her mouth to speak, but the words did not come. She could only stand and wait.

She felt tears fill her eyes because she could not answer, and her heart cried.

(31)

"Oho," he said. "I see a story here. The tree grows beside your rice field, and it will die because there is no water in the field. And since you bring this painting to me, my House is concerned with this. Is it possible that the canal on my land has not been opened to release the water to yours?"

Peach Blossom bowed three times, quickly, quickly.

"Was this the message that your brother left on the written scroll?"

She smiled.

He nodded his head wisely. "Now this is what comes of being a dullard," he said. "None in my house can read. When I was a child at the age of learning, I was sickly and was not taught. And often have I regretted it.

"Then it was your father and brother who came upon the land before the rising of the sun, trying only to free the water."

He clapped his hands, and a fat man came shuffling into the garden.

The neighbor spoke to the man kindly.

"You have said that thieves came in the early morning. This is not so. Our neighbors from the south came only to free the water that it might run into their fields. See to this at once. He turned toward Peach Blossom.

"It is well when one neighbor comes to another withour fear," he said.

And Peach Blossom was not afraid; she felt like singing—

As she hurried home, she saw that already the rice field was filling with the bubbling green river water.

Ho shouted as she came.

"We are ready for the planting. We are ready for the planting."

Her father looked at her curiously. "Where were you, Little Two?"

Little Two looked at him through her eyelashes.

"I went to our neighbor," she said softly.

She watched the transplanting.

Her father and Ho were ankle deep in the mud of the fields, when the neighbor from the north came; and his three men followed in single file behind him.

"Your unworthy neighbor has brought his unworthy men to help with the planting," he said.

They set to work together; and the three men labored with purpled faces and did the work of seven.

That day, Peach Blossom sewed with fine silk, and a tutor came to teach her to play upon the samisen.

She heard the men talking and laughing at their planting; the wind that blew across the rice fields was cool against her face.

(38)

When he came from the fields that night, her father said:

"Your picture accomplished more than words, Little Two. You have done well."

Peach Blossom put away her sticks of water color where she could find them again tomorrow, and with a small song on her lips, went to help her mother prepare the evening rice.

(39)

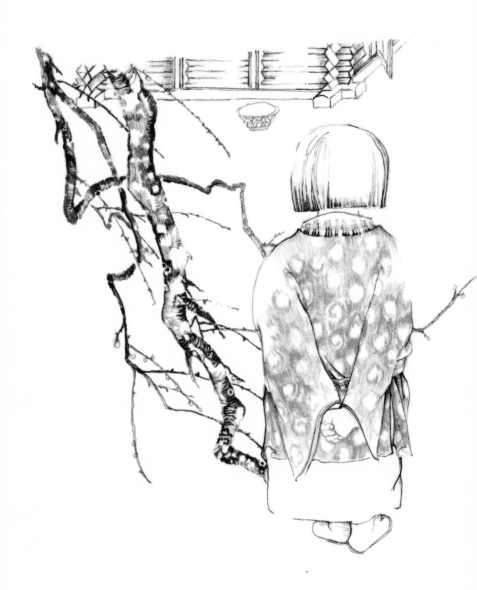